For Max and Mason

Bloomsbury Publishing, London, New Delhi, New York and Sydney

First Published in Great Britain in 2013 by Bloomsbury Publishing Plc
50 Bedford Square, London, WC1B 3DP

Text and illustrations copyright © Salina Yoon 2012

The moral right of the author/illustrator has been asserted

A CIP catalogue record for this book is available from the British Library

ISBN 978 1 4088 3906 5 (HB)
ISBN 978 1 4088 3907 2 (PB)

Printed in China by C&C Offset Printing Co., Ltd., Shenzhen, Guangdong

1 3 5 7 9 10 8 6 4 2

All papers used by Bloomsbury Publishing, Inc., are natural, recyclable products
made from wood grown in well-managed forests. The manufacturing processes
conform to the environmental regulations of the country of origin.

www.bloomsbury.com

Penguin on Holiday

Salina Yoon

BLOOMSBURY
LONDON NEW DELHI NEW YORK SYDNEY

'I need a holiday,'
Penguin sighed.

Penguin had skied,

sledged,

and skated on holidays before.

He wanted to go somewhere different.

Ninety-nine balls
of snow on the ground...

Somewhere . . .

'That's it! I'll go on holiday to the beach!' said Penguin.

Penguin packed his bag
and headed north.

The waves swelled bigger and bigger.

The sun shone hotter and hotter.

Finally, Penguin reached the beach.

It wasn't what Penguin expected.

— Ow!

Ow!

Ow!

The beach was nothing like his icy home.

Penguin learned some things.

You can't ski on sand.

You can't sledge on sand.

And you definitely can't skate on sand.

'Are you lost?' asked Crab.
'No, I'm on holiday,'
said Penguin.

'Then come with me!' said Crab.

Crab showed Penguin how
to have fun on the beach.

Sandcastle.

Penguin and Crab played . . .

and played . . .

and played.

Penguin loved his new friend.

But all holidays come to an end.

It was time for Penguin to go home.

The journey was long and quiet,

but suddenly, something moved
in the water.

'Crab? What are you doing here?'

'I need a holiday, too!' said Crab.

Penguin and Crab finally reached the shore.

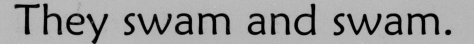

They swam and swam.

They whooshed and pushed.

They fished and wished.

But all holidays come to an end.
Crab set off for home

Goodbye, Crab.

. . . the sound of the beach.

'I shell return,' wrote Crab.

So Penguin waited.

And one day, Crab did!